The
I Believe
Bunny

By Tish Rabe

Illustrated By
Frank Endersby

THOMAS NELSON
Since 1798

NASHVILLE   DALLAS   MEXICO CITY   RIO DE JANEIRO   BEIJING

THE I BELIEVE BUNNY™ SERIES

Published in Nashville, Tennessee, by Thomas Nelson®. Thomas Nelson is a registered trademark of Thomas Nelson, Inc.

Literary agent: Patty Sullivan with p.s. ink publishing solutions

Illustrated by Frank Endersby

Thomas Nelson, Inc., titles may be purchased in bulk for educational, business, fund-raising, or sales promotional use. For information, please e-mail SpecialMarkets@ThomasNelson.com.

Library of Congress Cataloging-in-Publication Data

Rabe, Tish.
I Believe Bunny / by Tish Rabe ; illustrated by Frank Endersby.
p. cm.
Summary: Little Mouse is in trouble and Bunny is the only one nearby
to help, but he is small and unsure of himself until he starts to pray,
realizing that God can help him be strong.
ISBN 978-1-4003-1476-8 (hardcover)
[1. Stories in rhyme. 2. Faith—Fiction. 3. Rabbits—Fiction. 4. Mice—Fiction.] I. Endersby, Frank, ill. II. Title.
PZ8.3.R1145Iab 2009
[E]—dc22
2009000431

Printed in China

09 10 11 12 MT 6 5 4 3 2 1

I can do everything through him
who gives me strength.

PHILIPPIANS 4:13

Once upon a time
in a land hard to find
lived the I Believe Bunny,
who was funny and kind.

He thanked God for his home
in a flower-filled glen
where the sun shined a lot, but . . .

it rained now and then.

When it rained . . .
Bunny's whiskers got droopy,
and his ears lost their fluff.

He said to himself,
"It's been raining all morning.
I think that's enough!"

"Bunny, come play with us!"
said a bright butterfly.
"We'll find somewhere to go
that will be nice and dry."

"Thank you," he said.
"But I think I will stay.
I hope that the rain
will stop sometime today."

He felt soggy and boggy
and stuck to the ground.
But then he heard something . . .
a high, squeaky sound.

A small mouse was struggling
and calling to him.
"Please help me!" she cried.
"I don't know how to swim!"

She was caught in the river!
It was muddy and high.
Could Bunny reach her in time?
He knew he must try.

"Help us! Please help!" he called,
but no one was near.
He looked at the deep river
and shivered in fear.

He was just a small bunny.
So what could he do?
"Hold on!" Bunny called.
"I will try to help you!"

So, he pulled on a tree,
and he broke off a stick.
With no time to waste,
he would have to be quick!

He reached out to the mouse,
but he started to slip.
The water was rushing.
He was losing his grip!

Then he prayed to God, "Please,
can you help me right now?
I want to save this mouse,
but I don't know how."

Bunny was scared,
but he held on and prayed,
"God help me be strong
so she's not swept away!"

Then he heard someone calling,
"We're coming! Hold on tight!"
And he knew in his heart,
everything was all right.

God sent Bunny's friends,
Squirrel, Skunk, and Raccoon,
and together they rescued
the mouse very soon.

The sun started to shine.
God had answered his prayer.
"Thank you," said the mouse.
"I'm so glad you were there."

When Bunny needed help
and he stopped to pray,
he learned something true
on that rainy, spring day.

Have faith in God's love,
and you'll find when you do,
nothing you try will be
impossible for you.

Just like the I Believe Bunny,
you may get a surprise.
You CAN make a difference,
even a bunny . . .

your size.